Harry Potter

AND THE
HALF-BLOOD PRINCE™

MOVIE POSTER BOOK

SCHOLASTIC INC.

New York   Toronto   London   Auckland   Sydney
Mexico City   New Delhi   Hong Kong   Buenos Aires

DANIEL RADCLIFFE

DANIEL RADCLIFFE

THE BASICS

FULL NAME	DANIEL RADCLIFFE
HARRY POTTER CHARACTER	HARRY POTTER
BIRTHDAY	JULY 23
ASTROLOGICAL SIGN	ON THE CUSP OF CANCER AND LEO
EYES	BLUE
HAIR	DARK BROWN
RECENT TV CREDITS	*MY BOY JACK* (PBS)
RECENT NON-HP MOVIE CREDITS	*DECEMBER BOYS* (VILLAGE ROADSHOW/ WARNER BROS)
RECENT STAGE CREDITS	*EQUUS*—GIELGUD THEATRE, LONDON BROADHURST THEATRE, NEW YORK

Q & A

How do you feel *Harry Potter and the Half-Blood Prince* differs from the earlier movies?

Half-Blood Prince differs from the earlier movies in that as the characters and story lines have developed and changed, so have the films. In *Half-Blood Prince*, it is a film of extremes—the dark aspects are even darker than before, and the humor is even funnier. It will be an interesting film, seeing how these two extremes play against each other.

Are there specific traits you admire about your Harry Potter character?

I always admire anyone who is brave and stands up for what he believes—and that is what I admire about Harry.

What elements of your Harry Potter character have proven most challenging to play?

I think portraying Harry's grief at losing his parents, Sirius, and Dumbledore have been the most challenging aspects to portray.

DANIEL RADCLIFFE

What experiences have you drawn from in creating your character?

I have grown up playing Harry, so I think there are parallels in most teenage boys' lives, with feelings that are universal—e.g. first kiss, etc.—that I have been able to draw upon.

As an actor, does being strongly associated with your Harry Potter character ever present professional challenges?

No, playing Harry has done nothing but open doors for me and present me with the most interesting characters to play outside the Harry Potter world, from *Extras* with Ricky Gervais to Jack Kipling in *My Boy Jack* and Alan Strang in *Equus*.

How do you feel now when you watch the early Harry Potter movies? Does viewing the earlier films ever affect your current performance?

I never watch the earlier Potter films. For me, the most important part of the acting process is what is happening to you at that moment in time and not what has happened in the past, in previous films.

Daniel Radcliffe

Is there a particular acting challenge or story element that you are looking forward to dealing with in *Harry Potter and the Deathly Hallows*?

The biggest challenge in *Deathly Hallows* will be surviving the length of the shoot that it will take to fully realize the film. I see it as a Herculean task and one that I am relishing!!!

The Harry Potter movies often involve special effects. Is it hard to act against a green screen?

I have grown up with special effects and green screen, so it really isn't a problem to maintain the character of Harry. As always, it is about believing that an orange ball is [another character], and if I believe it, then the audience will as well.

As an actor, what other types of art do you find inspire you? Paintings? Novels? Classic films? Theatre?

As a person, I am extremely interested in all aspects of the arts and take inspiration from them all. If I had to choose one area I am particularly inspired by, it would have to be poetry or music.

DANIEL RADCLIFFE

If you could play a different Harry Potter character, which one would it be? Why?

I would definitely want to play Sirius Black. It would be fascinating to play him and to explore his relationship with Harry from the other perspective.

Which of the seven Harry Potter books is your favorite from a character or story perspective? Why?

My favorite book would be *Harry Potter and the Order of the Phoenix* because of the Sirius/Harry relationship. It marked a significant shift in Harry's character and it was, as always, a great experience working with Gary Oldman.

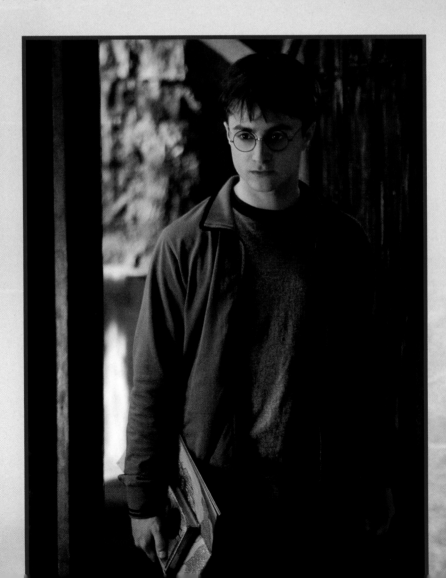

DANIEL RADCLIFFE

DANIEL FINISHES THE SENTENCE

If I weren't an actor . . . I would like to be a writer.

My most challenging scene in the Harry Potter films to date was . . . filming the death of Sirius Black.

My favorite moment shooting *Half-Blood Prince* was . . . doing anything with Michael Gambon.
He is an extraordinary actor and it is always highly entertaining to be around him.

EMMA WATSON

EMMA WATSON

THE BASICS

FULL NAME	**EMMA CHARLOTTE WATSON**
HARRY POTTER CHARACTER	**HERMIONE GRANGER**
BIRTHDAY	**APRIL 15**
ASTROLOGICAL SIGN	**ARIES**
EYES	**BROWN**
HAIR	**LIGHT BROWN**
RECENT TV CREDITS	***BALLET SHOES*** **(A BRITISH TV MOVIE)**

Q & A

How do you feel *Harry Potter and the Half-Blood Prince* differs from the earlier movies?

For me, *Half-Blood Prince* is much more of a romantic comedy.

Are there specific traits you admire about your Harry Potter character?

Her loyalty, her kindness, her braveness, and her brains.

What elements of your Harry Potter character have proven most challenging to play?

Hermione is quite an emotional character, and a worrier. I become much more introspective when I am stressed, upset, or worried.

What experiences have you drawn from in creating your character?

Hermione and I both love to learn, being in a school environment. I always pretend Harry is my younger brother Alex.

As an actor, does being strongly associated with your Harry Potter character ever present professional challenges?

Yes, typecasting worries me.

How do you feel now when you watch the early Harry Potter movies? Does viewing the earlier films ever affect your current performance?

No, I view each film as a new project. I draw on the books and my instincts. I try to learn and use the director as much as possible.

EMMA WATSON

Is there a particular acting challenge or story element that you are looking forward to dealing with in *Harry Potter and the Deathly Hallows*?

I am excited to get out of Hogwarts and be on the road. I have missed action in this film. I am already training for my stunts!

The Harry Potter movies often involve special effects. Is it hard to act against a green screen?

I have had a lot of practice over the years, although [watching] Quidditch is hard.

As an actor, what other types of art do you find inspire you? Paintings? Novels? Classic films? Theatre?

I am doing my Art A-level and I am inspired by art—poetry, plays, music.

If you could play a different Harry Potter character, which one would it be? Why?

Professor Umbridge, as her character is very complex and I see that as a challenge.

Which of the seven Harry Potter books is your favorite from a character or story perspective? Why?

Harry Potter and the Prisoner of Azkaban. Hermione was very integral to the moving on of the plot and part of the action and story.

EMMA FINISHES THE SENTENCE

If I weren't an actor . . . I would be in school!

My most challenging scene in the Harry Potter films to date was . . . the night shoots for Dumbledore's death scene. It was freezing and I had to keep focused!

My favorite moment shooting *Half-Blood Prince* was . . . turning eighteen on set and having all my friends to celebrate it with me!

RUPERT GRINT

RUPERT GRINT

THE BASICS

FULL NAME	**RUPERT GRINT**
HARRY POTTER CHARACTER:	**RON WEASLEY**
BIRTHDAY	**AUGUST 24**
ASTROLOGICAL SIGN	**VIRGO**
EYES	**GREEN**
HAIR	**RED**
RECENT NON-HP MOVIE CREDITS	*DRIVING LESSONS*

Q & A

How do you feel *Harry Potter and the Half-Blood Prince* differs from the earlier movies?

It's a little lighter, there's more comedy this time round—feels like a more mature, relationship-based movie.

Are there specific traits you admire about your Harry Potter character?

He's a loyal, friendly, easygoing, handsome redhead!

What elements of your Harry Potter character have proven most challenging to play?

I found the Quidditch sequences quite challenging; I'd always looked forward to it and was disappointed after missing out on *Order of the Phoenix*. (Editor's note: Although there are Quidditch scenes in the book, they were not included in the movie.) But after a month of sitting on a broom it wasn't as fun as I'd anticipated . . . more painful and time-consuming!

As an actor, does being strongly associated with your Harry Potter character ever present professional challenges?

Haven't found so yet; outside of shooting I'm always happy to be associated with Ron, but he's never followed me to another role.

How do you feel now when you watch the early Harry Potter movies? Does viewing the earlier films ever affect your current performance?

No, not really because there never seems to be time to watch the earlier films! Plus, it's too weird looking back at myself!

RUPERT GRINT

Is there a particular acting challenge or story element that you are looking forward to dealing with in *Harry Potter and the Deathly Hallows*?

Yeah, I'm quite looking forward to seeing how I'll look nineteen years on. I think the biggest challenge for me in the next film will be kissing Emma, as we've been good friends for eight years—it's going to be quite strange!

The Harry Potter movies often involve special effects. Is it hard to act against a green screen?

Yeah, that can be quite tricky, but it's something we've had to get used to over the years. It definitely helps to have a good imagination!

As an actor, what other types of art do you find inspire you? Paintings? Novels? Classic films? Theatre?

I really enjoy most forms of art, particularly painting and drawing, but I also really enjoy going to see live music.

If you could play a different Harry Potter character, which one would it be? Why?

I think Lupin would be most interesting as there are so many sides to his character—plus he gets to turn into a werewolf . . . .

Which of the seven Harry Potter books is your favorite from a character or story perspective? Why?

Harry Potter and the Goblet of Fire, because lots more characters arrived and different friendships were established outside of the main three.

RUPERT FINISHES THE SENTENCE

If I weren't an actor . . . I'd probably want to be a cartoonist, or something to do with art.

My most challenging scene in the Harry Potter films to date was . . . the spider test on rehearsals with a baby tarantula crawling up my leg, which was fortunately cut.

My favorite moment shooting *Half-Blood Prince* was . . . burning the Weasley house down.

TOM FELTON

Tom Felton

THE BASICS

FULL NAME	THOMAS ANDREW FELTON
HARRY POTTER CHARACTER	DRACO MALFOY
BIRTHDAY	SEPTEMBER 22
ASTROLOGICAL SIGN	VIRGO
EYES	BLUE
HAIR	UNCERTAIN . . . BROWNISH?!
RECENT NON-HP MOVIE CREDITS	*THE DISAPPEARED* (NOT YET RELEASED)

Q & A

How do you feel *Harry Potter and the Half-Blood Prince* differs from the earlier movies?

In earlier films, Hogwarts and Voldemort never met, and Harry's adventures seemed about one or the other. In this film, evil enters Hogwarts in unassuming ways, and even without Voldemort's presence, it feels darker!

Are there specific traits you admire about your Harry Potter character?

He's a slimy, posh, git! I love the way he speaks—I get to lay on the British accent pretty thick—that's about it!

What elements of your Harry Potter character have proven most challenging to play?

It was new to show Draco's vulnerable side, which proved challenging. In this film, in parts, he's very fragile and unstable . . . great fun acting.

What experiences have you drawn from in creating your character?

Being pushed around by my brothers . . .

As an actor, does being strongly associated with your Harry Potter character ever present professional challenges?

I haven't experienced any, but only the future will tell.

TOM FELTON

How do you feel now when you watch the early Harry Potter movies? Does viewing the earlier films ever affect your current performance?

No, I just can't believe how small we all were and how everyone has progressed soooo much!

Is there a particular acting challenge or story element that you are looking forward to dealing with in *Harry Potter and the Deathly Hallows*?

Our final battle in the Room of Requirement will be great fun! I'm looking forward to Harry saving my life.

The Harry Potter movies often involve special effects. Is it hard to act against a green screen?

We were all brought up around it, so it feels normal.

As an actor, what other types of art do you find inspire you? Paintings? Novels? Classic films? Theatre?

Other films, obviously, and music. I'm obsessed with the idea of leaving something behind, so recording, whether music or film, feels hugely satisfying.

If you could play a different Harry Potter character, which one would it be? Why?

I love Filch! He's pure comedy, and although I couldn't touch David Bradley's performance, it would be great fun.

Which of the seven Harry Potter books is your favorite from a character or story perspective? Why?

Harry Potter and the Half-Blood Prince, it has to be. Draco really gets a chance to show many sides of evildoings, which I hope should be interesting to watch. Story-wise, I love the *Chamber of Secrets* (the Basilisk does it for me!!).

TOM FINISHES THE SENTENCE

If I weren't an actor . . . **I'd be a struggling musician.**

My most challenging scene in the Harry Potter films to date was . . . **the bathroom scene in** *Half-Blood Prince.* **Tiring but fun.**

My favorite moment shooting *Half-Blood Prince* was . . . **falling in love with film and life . . . .**

BONNIE WRIGHT

BONNIE WRIGHT

THE BASICS

FULL NAME	**BONNIE FRANCESCA WRIGHT**
HARRY POTTER CHARACTER	**GINNY WEASLEY**
BIRTHDAY	**FEBRUARY 17**
ASTROLOGICAL SIGN	**AQUARIUS**
EYES	**BLUE**
HAIR	**AUBURN**

Q & A

How do you feel *Harry Potter and the Half-Blood Prince* differs from the earlier movies?

It effectively balances the humor of Hogwarts with the deepening seriousness of Lord Voldemort. There is also a sense that the end is near.

Are there specific traits you admire about your Harry Potter character?

Her optimism and her care and interest in others.

What experiences have you drawn from in creating your character?

My own life and growing up as a teenager.

How do you feel now when you watch the early Harry Potter movies? Does viewing the earlier films ever affect your current performance?

It is odd looking at how much the character has progressed, but it is useful to see how it has occurred. Ginny's experiences in *Harry Potter and the Chamber of Secrets* illustrate how she can relate to Harry, as she has also experienced being possessed by Lord Voldemort.

Is there a particular acting challenge or story element that you are looking forward to dealing with in *Harry Potter and the Deathly Hallows*?

It will be interesting to play Ginny as a more comfortable and confident character within situations. I cannot wait to explore the feisty and competitive attitude she has toward Quidditch.

BONNIE WRIGHT

The Harry Potter movies often involve special effects. Is it hard to act against a green screen?

Luckily, they always show us the artwork or footage that will be filled in so we can imagine ourselves there.

As an actor, what other types of art do you find inspire you? Paintings? Novels? Classic films? Theatre?

I love watching classic films and going to the theatre.

If you could play a different Harry Potter character, which one would it be? Why?

I think maybe someone with a vast physical contrast and someone more visually magic . . . maybe Hagrid.

Which of the seven Harry Potter books is your favorite from a character or story perspective? Why?

I have never been able to choose; I love all of them.

BONNIE FINISHES THE SENTENCE

If I weren't an actor . . . I would like to go to film or art school.

My most challenging scene in the Harry Potter films to date was . . . the death of Dumbledore and lying unconscious in the Chamber of Secrets.

My favorite moment shooting *Half-Blood Prince* was . . . the night shoot in the reeds surrounding the Weasley house . . . also, inside Weasley's Wizard Wheezes.

JAMES AND OLIVER PHELPS

JAMES AND OLIVER PHELPS

THE BASICS

	James Phelps	Oliver Phelps
Full Name	James Phelps	Oliver Phelps
Harry Potter Character	Fred Weasley	George Weasley
Birthday	February 25	February 25
Astrological Sign	Pisces	Pisces
Eyes	Brown	Hazel
Hair	Brown (Ginger For Days Being Fred)	Brown / Ginger

Q & A

How do you feel *Harry Potter and the Half-Blood Prince* differs from the earlier movies?

James: The cast have been together for eight years now, so we all know how each other works. The story has gotten darker and there are more and more things going on, but there is also more humor in this film than the others. I have been working every day in the Assistant Director's department so have now seen how everything works from the "other side."

Oliver: I think that the *Half-Blood Prince* is darker and you see how Voldemort's contingent is growing bigger and bigger. The plot is thickening and some pieces of the puzzle are fitting together.

Are there specific traits you admire about your Harry Potter character?

James: I always wish that I was as outgoing as Fred at his age. I also think his selling/business mind is something I would want!

Oliver: I like how George is very loyal to the cause of fighting [Dark] magic and helping his family.

What elements of your Harry Potter character have proven most challenging to play?

James: Being ginger . . . only kidding! I guess having to be very outgoing, as I am not initially like that.

Oliver: Definitely the dancing for the ball in *Harry Potter and the Goblet of Fire*.

What experiences have you drawn from in creating your character?

James: Having my hair dyed really did help, as it separates Fred from me. But also being able to learn how to dance; in the fourth film, we had to learn the waltz.

Oliver: When I used to mess about with James (my brother) when we were kids.

JAMES FINISHES THE SENTENCE

If I weren't an actor . . . I would either be a software designer (as I like my computers) or have a trade (plumber, carpenter, plasterer) as I like to get my hands stuck into something.

My most challenging scene in the Harry Potter films to date was . . . the Weasley joke shop. It took me a few moments to grasp the idea that I was in charge of a store! Fortunately all the crew were great and the cast all had a laugh when shooting it.

My favorite moment shooting *Half-Blood Prince* was . . . when we were shooting the Weasley house on fire. It was about 2:30 AM, we only had a few minutes left to get the shot, we all had to be in a sad state of mind . . . when Rupert got the giggles, which of course got me going, too. It has been like that from the first film, but somehow we managed to get the shot!

JAMES AND OLIVER PHELPS

As an actor, does being strongly associated with your Harry Potter character ever present professional challenges?

James: I don't feel so. I leave the character of Fred on the set at the end of the day and pick up the next day.

Oliver: It can. I think that this will always be the case with many people associated with projects as big as this.

How do you feel now when you watch the early Harry Potter movies? Does viewing the earlier films ever affect your current performance?

James: No . . . they are kind of like old family movies, in the sense that you see a young you on the screen. It was a shock the other day when I was flicking through the channels and the third film was on.

Oliver: I think it does to a certain degree. You definitely need to reflect on past experiences to grow your character and yourself as an actor.

Is there a particular acting challenge or story element that you are looking forward to dealing with in *Harry Potter and the Deathly Hallows*?

James: The final battle (for obvious reasons to those who have read it). I think that's what Fred will be remembered for, so I'm looking forward to the challenge of acting that out.

Oliver: Yes. Without spoiling the story, there is one scene I will be "listening" out for.

The Harry Potter movies often involve special effects. Is it hard to act against a green screen?

James: You just have to go back and use your imagination like when you were a child. It's always great to see the fantastic effects when we see the final cut.

Oliver: You get an idea of what you are dealing with before you do the scene. The crew will normally show you an animation of how they want the scene to look like. This was always the case when we were doing the Quidditch on the earlier films.

As an actor, what other types of art do you find inspire you?

James: Music. I am a huge music fan. I go to two or three festivals a year. I mostly like rock (on pretty much all levels except emo, I'm not really into that), but my iPod goes from Louis Armstrong and Ray Charles to AC/DC and Metallica.

Oliver: Although I am certainly no art buff, some paintings definitely inspire me. When I was younger, I was lucky enough to see an exhibit that had "The Scream" by Edvard Munch. It made me realize that I am lucky enough to live in a bright happy place, but others don't.

If you could play a different Harry Potter character, which one would it be? Why?

James: Well, I guess the obvious one would be George, as he's similar (but not as cool) as Fred! I think Voldemort, mainly as he's the bad guy and they are always fun to play.

Oliver: I would say I would like to play Professor Snape because he is such a complex character.

Which of the seven Harry Potter books is your favorite? Why?

James: I would say it's between *Goblet of Fire* and *Deathly Hallows*, as Fred has some very cool parts to do. I could not put either of them down when reading them, and I guess that's the sign of a good book.

Oliver: From a character point of view, it would certainly be the *Half-Blood Prince* because George and Fred open up Weasleys' Wizard Wheezes. They become entrepreneurs, which is good to see as the Weasley family haven't had much money.

OLIVER FINISHES THE SENTENCE

If I weren't an actor . . . **I would more than likely have gone to university and studied geology.**

My most challenging scene in the Harry Potter films to date was . . . **in the *Goblet of Fire*, George and Fred try and enter the Triwizard Tournament. We had to be pulled back on a harness and then have a fight . . . dressed as old men.**

My favorite moment shooting *Half-Blood Prince* was . . . **all the banter behind the scenes. Like beating James and Rupert at table tennis and all the jokes that go on.**

JESSIE CAVE

JESSIE CAVE

THE BASICS

FULL NAME	JESSIE CAVE
HARRY POTTER CHARACTER	LAVENDER BROWN
BIRTHDAY	MAY 5
ASTROLOGICAL SIGN	TAURUS
EYES	BLUE
HAIR	BLONDE (DARK)
RECENT TV CREDITS	*SUMMERHILL* (A BBC PRODUCTION)

Q & A

How do you feel *Harry Potter and the Half-Blood Prince* differs from the earlier movies?

The darker, colder undercurrent and budding romances.

Are there specific traits you admire about your Harry Potter character?

Lavender's gutsy determination in pursuit of Ron: she will not give up! And her true, honest besottedness with him.

The Harry Potter movies often involve special effects. Is it hard to act against a green screen?

Slightly tricky; it can be hard not to laugh when you think about what you are actually doing, which is usually reacting to a stick!

As an actor, what other types of art do you find inspire you?

I write and illustrate children's stories and have studied art. Live theater is so exhilarating, and a good character from any book can be referred to forever and ever and still be brilliant and inspiring.

If you could play a different Harry Potter character, which one would it be? Why?

Moaning Myrtle: what fun! Or Bellatrix . . .

Which of the seven Harry Potter books is your favorite from a character or story? Why?

The first, because of the memories I associate with that period of time, and also the sixth, because I can't believe I am playing Lavender Brown!

JESSIE FINISHES THE SENTENCE

If I weren't an actor . . . I'd be a writer or illustrator.

My most challenging scene in the Harry Potter films to date was . . . the hospital scene: the presence of such iconic actors was a tad nerve-wracking.

My favorite moment shooting *Half-Blood Prince* was . . . kissing Ron, of course!

EVANNA LYNCH

EVANNA LYNCH

THE BASICS

FULL NAME	**EVANNA LYNCH**
HARRY POTTER CHARACTER	**LUNA LOVEGOOD**
BIRTHDAY	**AUGUST 16**
ASTROLOGICAL SIGN	**LEO**
EYES	**BLUE**
HAIR	**BLONDE**

Q & A

How do you feel *Harry Potter and the Half-Blood Prince* differs from the earlier movies?

Although it has such a great balance of light and dark, I feel that the overall tone is much heavier. Throughout the first five books there is this constant threat of danger and of Voldemort's showing up at any odd moment. Because of this, Harry maintains his fighting spirit and instills that in others.

However, at the end of *Order of the Phoenix*, that element of knowledge vanishes when Dumbledore unveils the prophecy to Harry. It becomes fact to Harry that whether he likes it or not, he has to kill or be killed by Voldemort. Other than that the book is different because Ron and Hermione finally start playing up the drama, which they really should have done five books ago!

Are there specific traits you admire about your Harry Potter character?

Yes, many. I think she is a very balanced, well-rounded person and far wiser than her age would imply. I love her detachment, how she never needs approval from other people. She is not cocky, nor is she insecure, but just comfortable enough in her own mind not to let others' opinions affect her judgment. She listens to her own heart.

What elements of your Harry Potter character have proven most challenging to play?

I think that would just be her consistent positivity. It's hard to accept that someone can be so adjusted to life and its problems, and to death too. During the filming of *Order of the Phoenix* . . . I had trouble in the Ministry scenes where she had to be terrified of the Death Eaters. I couldn't see her terror when the worst thing that could happen to her was death. But we resolved it by saying the terror she felt was for her friends' lives.

What experiences have you drawn from in creating your character?

I think I've had to learn to be more detached. I am sensitive and when you spend your time desperately seeking others' approval, you always end up getting hurt and then worse off. Being in the public eye and knowing other people will judge you a lot has made me learn to only ever rely on what *I think* of what I am doing.

As an actor, does being strongly associated with your Harry Potter character ever present professional challenges?

Not so far, no. But I definitely don't call myself an "actor." I do want to act more, but I was in Harry Potter first and am grateful for everything I've got from it. I find it only opens doors for me.

How do you feel now when you watch the early Harry Potter movies? Does viewing the earlier films ever affect your current performance?

Honestly, no. Luna wasn't part of those stories and there's nothing in them that makes me have to change her to fit. I grew up watching them before filming Luna, so whether they affected my thinking on a subconscious level I can't be sure. I'm glad there are four other films where I can watch and enjoy as a fan again!

EVANNA LYNCH

Is there a particular acting challenge or story element that you are looking forward to dealing with in *Harry Potter and the Deathly Hallows*?

I think it will be Malfoy Manor, as that is quite a frightening experience for Luna and she has to show a lot of her Gryffindor side (yes, I do believe everyone has a Gryffindor side!) and take responsibility in ways she hasn't really had to do on her own before. It's a real test for her and I still am not quite sure how she will go about it . . . and I am excited to discover!

The Harry Potter movies often involve special effects. Is it hard to act against a green screen?

It certainly is odd. You go on set all ready for the scene to take off, but that just can't happen when you're surrounded by blinding acid green color and there's a man brandishing a pole with a red X right next to you. It is quite off-putting. However, it's just one of those things where you have to totally detach yourself from everyone around you who's laughing at the way you're gazing lovingly at the metal pole.

You just go into your own world, like when you were seven years old, and make what you imagine real.

As an actor, what other types of art do you find inspire you?

Everything! I couldn't limit myself to just one form of art. You never know and can't help what you're inspired by; I want to see all of it! Films, books, they all do it. I think dancing and movement are my passions, though.

If you could play a different Harry Potter character, which one would it be? Why?

Dumbledore! I love him! He's not unlike Luna in many ways . . . But Dumbledore is different in that he has so many worries and struggles that in a way make him more human. I think I would enjoy the challenge of trying to create a balance between his quirky detachedness and serene wisdom. Plus, I love his robes!

EVANNA FINISHES THE SENTENCE

If I weren't an actor . . . I'd be in school right now! But no, I would be a dancer. I want to keep acting, but I think I'd like to make dancing my career . . . it changes every week, though . . . .

My most challenging scene in the Harry Potter films to date was . . . the Ministry stuff. Green screens and SFX—it's hard not to feel a little foolish screaming "Stupefy" at thin air!

My favorite moment shooting *Half-Blood Prince* was . . . one of the Great Hall days, on Valentine's Day. People were bored waiting around on set, so Alfie (Enoch, who plays Dean Thomas) and Afshan (Azad, who plays Padma Patil) got out a laptop and learned the "Thriller" routine from YouTube and proceeded to teach the rest of the cast. That was something to see!

MATTHEW LEWIS

Matthew Lewis

The Basics

Full Name	Matthew David Lewis
Harry Potter Character	Neville Longbottom
Birthday	June 27
Astrological Sign	Cancer
Eyes	Green
Hair	Brown
TV Credits	*Heartbeat* (1999); *Where the Heart Is* (1996); *Dalziel & Pascoe* (1995); *Some Kind of Life* (1995)

Q & A

How do you feel *Harry Potter and the Half-Blood Prince* differs from the earlier movies?

Well, when filming we all have the same amount of fun and laughter as always, if not more, because as the years pass we get to know each other better.

Are there specific traits you admire about your Harry Potter character?

His endearing belief that he has to stand by his friends and do the right thing regardless of personal danger. I love his courage.

What elements of your Harry Potter character have proven most challenging to play?

He's very troubled. What happened to his parents hit him hard when he was younger. That's difficult to convey, but the script makes it easier for me!

What experiences have you drawn from in creating your character?

When I was younger and had just begun high school, I wasn't the most confident person. I was easily embarrassed and would panic if there was too much pressure, a bit like Neville.

As an actor, does being strongly associated with your Harry Potter character ever present professional challenges?

My main challenge after Harry Potter is to convince people that I'm more than Neville. If I get the chance, then I'm confident.

How do you feel now when you watch the early Harry Potter movies?

Can't do it! Watch once and never again, it's cringe-worthy.

Is there a particular acting challenge or story element that you are looking forward to dealing with in *Harry Potter and the Deathly Hallows*?

Having my head set on fire (when Voldemort puts the Sorting Hat on Neville's head). I doubt they'll let me do it, but I'd love to try.

Matthew Finishes the Sentence

If I weren't an actor . . . I'd like to think I'd join the army.

My most challenging scene in the Harry Potter films to date was . . . the scene when Neville explained what happened to his parents to Harry in the Room of Requirement.

My favorite moment shooting *Half-Blood Prince* was . . . beating Alfie (Enoch) 6-0 at darts, scoring my first 180, and checking out a leg with a 132 finish . . . what a day! Alfie was seething!